HIRO

Based on *The Railway Ser...*

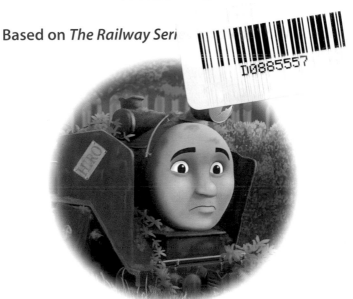

Illustrations by
Robin Davies

EGMONT

EGMONT

We bring stories to life

First published in Great Britain 2010
by Egmont UK Limited
239 Kensington High Street, London W8 6SA

Thomas the Tank Engine & Friends™

CREATED BY BRITT ALLCROFT

Based on the Railway Series by the Reverend W Awdry
© 2010 Gullane (Thomas) LLC. A HIT Entertainment company.
Thomas the Tank Engine & Friends and Thomas & Friends are trademarks of Gullane (Thomas) Limited.
Thomas the Tank Engine & Friends and Design is Reg. U.S. Pat. & Tm. Off.

HiT entertainment

ISBN 978 1 4052 5112 9
1 3 5 7 9 10 8 6 4 2
Printed in Italy

FSC

Mixed Sources
Product group from well-managed
forests and other controlled sources

Cert no. TT-COC-002332
www.fsc.org
© 1996 Forest Stewardship Council

Egmont is passionate about helping to preserve the world's remaining ancient forests. We only use paper from legal and sustainable forest sources.

This book is made from paper certified by the Forestry Stewardship Council (FSC), an organisation dedicated to promoting responsible management of forest resources. For more information on the FSC, please visit www.fsc.org. To learn more about Egmont's sustainable paper policy, please visit www.egmont.co.uk/ethical

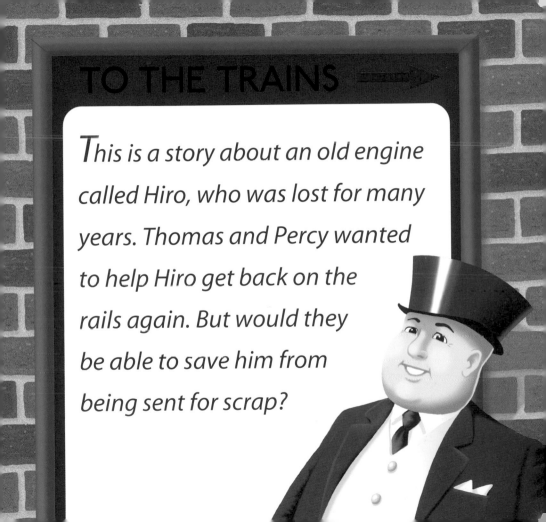

This is a story about an old engine called Hiro, who was lost for many years. Thomas and Percy wanted to help Hiro get back on the rails again. But would they be able to save him from being sent for scrap?

One summer, Spencer was visiting the Island of Sodor. He was helping build a summer house for the Duke and Duchess of Boxford.

"Out of my way, slowcoach! I've no time to chat," he would say. He boasted that he was the fastest and the strongest engine on Sodor.

One day, Spencer challenged Thomas to a contest to see who was strongest. "Whoever pulls his heavy load the furthest wins," he sneered.

Thomas and Spencer met at the Shunting Yards. Edward whistled, "Peep! Peep!" and they were off!

Spencer steamed ahead. But little Thomas was soon in trouble. At the top of a steep hill, he felt that something was wrong.

"My brakes have broken, I'm going too fast!" Thomas gasped. He whooshed down the other side of the hill on to an old rickety track.

He crashed through some bushes and came to a stop.

Just then, a voice called, "Hello?" Thomas was surprised to see an old engine. He looked rusty and broken.

"My name is Hiro," said the engine.

"What are you doing here?" Thomas asked.

Hiro told Thomas how he had come to Sodor from far away. "I was the strongest engine there," said Hiro, proudly. "They called me 'the Master of the Railway'."

Thomas promised to fix Hiro and make him as good as new.

Thomas was so excited that he forgot all about Spencer.

He puffed slowly to the Sodor Steamworks to get his brakes fixed. His friend Victor was there.

Thomas saw a wagon with an old boiler. "What's going to happen to that, Victor?" asked Thomas.

"That rubbish? It's just scrap," said Victor.

Thomas offered to take it away. "This boiler could be mended and given to Hiro!" thought Thomas.

That night in the Sheds, Thomas told Percy all about his new friend, Hiro.

Thomas made Percy promise not to tell anyone. "If The Fat Controller finds out, he might send Hiro for scrap," Thomas worried.

So Thomas and Percy made a plan. The next morning, Percy hid his mail trucks and worked on Thomas' branch line so that Thomas and his crew could start fixing Hiro.

Nosy Spencer wondered what they were up to!

On his way back home that evening, Thomas saw Percy looking sad. "I burst a valve pulling the load on your branch line," Percy moaned.

Thomas felt sorry for his friend, and shunted Percy to the Steamworks. Just then, The Fat Controller arrived. He was very cross.

"Thomas! Why was Percy pulling your carriages instead of delivering the mail?" he boomed. "And where are his mail trucks?"

Thomas felt terrible. He promised to help Percy with the mail train the next morning.

At Tidmouth Sheds, the engines wanted to know why Thomas was in trouble with The Fat Controller.

Thomas huffed a huge puff. He needed his friends' help, so he told them all about Hiro. "When Hiro broke down, his crew couldn't find the parts to fix him, so he was put in a siding and everyone forgot about him," Thomas said.

Gordon gasped! And James jumped! All the engines wanted to help Hiro.

The next few days were very busy on Sodor. Gordon, Edward and James took it in turns to carry parts to Hiro. And Thomas worked on his branch line.

But little Percy had forgotten where he had hidden his mail trucks.

Thomas and Percy decided to visit Hiro and look for the missing trucks later.

"Look at me!" cried Hiro, as his firebox began to flare. Hiro was a colourful patchwork of parts, and he was feeling better already.

Suddenly there came a loud, "Poop! Poop!" It was Spencer! When he saw Hiro, he gasped.

"So this is what you've been doing!" he smirked. "Making a heap of scrap for the Smelter's Yard. Wait until I tell The Fat Controller." And with that, Spencer wheeshed away.

Thomas had to tell The Fat Controller about Hiro before Spencer did! He pumped his pistons and soon caught up with the big engine.

Then the old track gave way under big Spencer and he got stuck wheel-deep in mud!

Thomas puffed on to Knapford Station, his wheels whirring. He told The Fat Controller everything . . . about Hiro and how he didn't want him to be scrapped, and about Spencer, who was stuck in the mud.

"Did you say Hiro?" asked The Fat Controller. "He was the Master of the Railway! Why would I scrap him? You should have told me before."

The Fat Controller ordered Hiro to be taken to the Steamworks straight away.

A few days later, Hiro had a brand new boiler, a shiny funnel and a proper coat of paint. He looked splendid!

Spencer was still stuck in the mud – Percy and Thomas weren't strong enough to pull him out. But Hiro was.

With a mighty heave, Hiro lifted Spencer on to the tracks and took him to the Steamworks.

"Thank you, Hiro," said Spencer, in a sorry voice.

One morning, all the engines gathered at the Docks to say goodbye to Hiro.

"It's time for you to go home," said Thomas.

"I will never forget how you saved me. Do come and visit me one day," chuffed Hiro.

The engines whistled as Hiro puffed on to the ship.

The rest of the summer on Sodor went more smoothly. Percy found his mail trucks and Thomas helped Spencer finish the summer house for the Duke and Duchess. And they never forgot about Hiro, the Master of the Railway.

Two Great Offers for Thomas Fans!

In every Thomas Story Library book like this one, you will find a special token. Collect the tokens and claim exclusive Thomas goodies:

Offer 1

Collect 6 tokens and we'll send you a **poster** and a **bookmark** for only **£1**. (to cover P&P)

1 THOMAS TOKEN

offer 2

Collect 12 tokens and we'll send you a **choo-choo-tastic book bag** for only **£2.**
(to cover P&P)

Visit **www.egmont.co.uk/thomaslibrary** for more special offers, games and competitions!

Simply tape a £1 or £2 coin in the space above, and fill in the form overleaf.

The Thomas bag contains 7 specially designed pockets to hold Thomas Story Library books. Please note that the books featured in the picture above are not included in the offer.

Reply Card for Thomas Goodies!

1 Yes, please send me a **Thomas poster and bookmark.**
I have enclosed **6 tokens plus a £1 coin** to cover P&P. ☐

2 Yes, please send me a **Thomas book bag.**
I have enclosed **12 tokens plus £2** to cover P&P. ☐

Simply fill in your details below and send them to:
Thomas Offers, PO BOX 715, Horsham, RH 12 5WG

Fan's Name: ....

Address: ....

....

.... Date of Birth: ....

Email: ....

Name of parent/guardian: ....

Signature of parent/guardian: ....

Please allow 28 days for delivery. Offer is only available while stocks last. We reserve the right to change the terms of this offer at any time and we offer a 14 day money back guarantee. This does not affect your statutory rights. Offer applies to UK only. The cost applies to Postage and Packaging (P&P).

We may occasionally wish to send you information about other Egmont children's books but if you would rather we didn't please tick here ☐